# LOGAN'S JOURNEY TO CHRIST

## HOPE BRYAN

*AuthorHouse*™
*1663 Liberty Drive*
*Bloomington, IN 47403*
*www.authorhouse.com*
*Phone: 1 (800) 839-8640*

*Published by AuthorHouse 08/03/2016*

*ISBN: 978-1-5246-1909-1 (sc)*
*ISBN: 978-1-5246-1905-3 (e)*
*ISBN: 978-1-5246-1908-4 (h)*

*Library of Congress Control Number: 2016911624*

*Print information available on the last page.*

*Any people depicted in stock imagery provided by Thinkstock are models,*
*and such images are being used for illustrative purposes only.*
*Certain stock imagery © Thinkstock.*

*Th is book is printed on acid-free paper.*

*Because of the dynamic nature of the Internet, any web addresses or links contained in this book may have changed*
*since publication and may no longer be valid. The views expressed in this work are solely those of the author and do not*
*necessarily reflect the views of the publisher, and the publisher hereby disclaims any responsibility for them.*

authorHOUSE®

# LOGAN's JOURNEY TO CHRIST

## HOPE BRYAN

Once upon a time there was a girl named Latoya. Her brother saw that she was sad and because he loved her so much and wanted to cheer her up, he got her a puppy. Adam, her brother, got the puppy from a junk yard off a street named Logan, in Philadelphia, so he named the puppy "Logan".

Latoya was a christian girl, so she would read the bible to him from he was a pup, singing gospel songs to him, ministering to him, and even laying hands on him. One day, Latoya kidding to herself, said to Logan, "There is nothing else I can teach you except to talk."

A miracle happened and Logan spoke and said, "If you believe, you will receive whatever you ask for in prayer." (Matthew 21:22). "If you have faith as small as a mustard seed, you can say to the mountain move from here to there and it will move." (Matthew 17:20). His faith grew and grew. Logan said, once he started hearing the word of God, he knew that without faith it would be impossible for him to please God.

Logan said, "I understand if we believe in Jesus all things are possible." So Latoya asked again, "How is this possible?" Logan replied, "It was as if he was being transformed into a new creation from the inside out." He was still a dog he said, but all the woof woof started turning into "praise the Lord, thank you Jesus, and Hallelujah". Logan said, "The bible says my people perish for a lack of knowledge about God, and that knowledge was given to me through you, my master Latoya. Hearing the word has brought changes into my life. Suddenly I know from you reading the Bible that God wanted to have a relationship with me, and by me having a relationship with him, I can talk to him about anything."

In amazement, Latoya asked for the final time, "How are you talking?" Logan replied, "The Bible says to make your request known, so I did. And it also says in (1 John 1:9), If we confess our sins He is faithful and just to forgive us for our sins and to cleanse us from all unrighteousness. So, I told Jesus all the things I did bad. For example, how I peed on your plant in the dining room a couple of times when you were not home, and I peed in your bed when I was upset with you."

"I told Jesus I was sorry abut knocking down your christmas tree and eating all the candy canes off the tree but they were so delicious. I told Jesus I was sorry for biting and putting holes in all the room doors. I said sorry Lord and please forgive me. After confessing my sins, I felt like I was free and shortly after that I was able to speak words."

"In order for God to answer my prayers I had to stop sinning and repent so I did. I stop sinning and I turned to Jesus daily. That means I had to stop chasing cars, cats, and mice and do what Latoya tells me to do, like getting the newspaper, sitting when you say sit, speaking when you say speak, and no fighting with my brother King."

"I felt a peace come over me. I trust the Lord with all my heart and I know He will direct my path into my new journey."


THE END

Thank you so much.

Printed in the United States
by Baker & Taylor Publisher Services